Dark Fears

A Series of Short Horror Stories

By: Jennifer Valdez

Dedicated to my nephew Aramis, keep loving horror like your aunt. Horror nerds are awesome! Love you kid!

Stories

Something Went Wrong

People always told me ..
"Don't ever play with a Ouija Board if you
don't know what you're doing"
I don't always pay attention to what people tell
me; I do what I want when I want.
Sometimes I should just listen.. I should of listened
..

Years ago, when I was in high school, my friends
and I decided to go into a Botanica, you know,
those places where they sell candles and those
potions where u can make someone "fall in love"
with you, yea one of those places just to look
around and see what the big deal was . My
grandma was always going into these places
and coming home with weird stuff like bead
necklaces and Saints. She use to sit late at night
at an altar she had full of candles and Saints and
just speak to them and pray before going to
bed.
I always thought it was weird but never bothered
to ask why she did it.
I felt because of the things she did.. along with
my God mother, I felt that my apartment, the
one I grew up in, was always weird. It felt strange
and odd like something didn't belong there. My
cousin and I always saw dark shadow's late at
night, heard whispers and saw doors opening by
themselves. It was super creepy. Luckily things

happened when my cousin and I were together.

I walked around the Botanica not so sure what I was exacly looking for. I walked the isles back and forth, smelling the different fragrances and admiring the colorful items on the shelves, until I walked into an Isle that seemed pretty isolated from the others. It smelled damped. It was dark, gloomy with cobwebs. It was surrounded by old boxes and black and white candles with candle wax running down them. Towards the back of the Isle there was a table covered with a black, fairly new table cloth.

On top of the table cloth were two white candles fairly used, a glass of water and a small black book. In the middle of the table was a board. It had letters in the middle and numbers on the bottom on it. The words "Yes" and "No" were on the top coners with the moon and the sun drawn on them and the words goodbye at the very bottom. There was also this triangular piece above the board with a circular glass in the middle.
I got closer to the board and recognized what it was.. it was a Ouija Board.

"I've seen this before" I thought to myself..

I heard a noise behind me .. I turned around and it was one of my friends.. Rebeca..

"Dude, look at this" Rebeca said

She had a small book in her hand. The words on the cover read.. Black Magic..
I looked at her and smiled .
"Look what I found"
I showed her the table and she freaked out. She started backing away, her face went pale.

"Rebeca what's wrong?!" I asked her
"That's a Ouija Board.. I heard so many bad things about that board, never thought I would be face to face with one. It just gave me the creeps"

I looked at her. She didn't like the look on my face. I was smiling.
I told her I wanted to buy it.

"ARE YOU INSANE?!"
"Do you understand how dangerous that thing is?" She asked me with a concern look on her face.

I didn't care. I just wanted to buy it. I wanted to experience this thing again. I wanted to see if it was still real.

Yea I forgot to mention . . I had one before. My friends and I experienced something terrifying but I honestly thought it was fake. They were lying to me just to scare me. It worked though but now I want to see if this thing really works.

"Come on Rebeca, I'm just going to see if it really works. How about I don't buy it and we try it out here in the botanica. What's the worst that can happen? This place is suppose to be protected and it looks like it was being used anyway." I expressed

"Dude I can't, I'm a Christian." Rebeca said

"Omg, I've seen Christians do worst, cut it out, you're gonna try this with me and that's it. Go get the other ones." I responded

Rebeca rolled her eyes and walked away to get the others.
I inspected the board. Making sure that it was

real. I believe it was. It was actually made out of wood, even the planchette, that's what the little triangle with the glass in the middle was called. Looks like someone was using it already. I wonder who and why. As I kept inspecting the board I felt a chill on the back of my neck. Goosebumps all over my body. I looked behind me but I just saw my friends walking my way. As they walked I decided to sit on a chair that was by the table where the Ouija board laid.

"Come guys, come sit with me"

"Oooohhhh snaaappp... it's a Witch board" (another name for the Ouija Board).. Diana, who has been my best friend all my life, was excited to see it.

"It's about to go down" William, my trusty chaotic side kick exclaimed.

"Oh boy, here we go" Rebeca sat next to me shaking her head.

"Ok guys before we even do this, let's say a prayer. I don't wanna start without one, just in case something does really happen"

"What's gonna happen?!" Rebeca asked
"Nothing because you're going to pray for us" I

told her .

"Why I gotta pray?! She asked

"Cause you're the church girl and the most chicken" I smirked

She just looked at me and rolled her eyes.
"Hold hands and bow your heads, let's get this over with already"

We all looked at each other one last time before praying. I felt a chill but I knew that was just me bugging out. As Rebeca prayed, I took a peek at everyone. They all had their heads bowed low, listening to her words. At that moment I thought to myself, my friends are so cool, I wouldn't replace them for the world.

"Dear God, please don't be mad at what we're about to do and let us come out of this alive.."

"Really Rebz? We're not gonna die" Diana said

"Shh, who's praying me or you?"

Part 2

We prayed..

"Ok guys, put your fingertips on the planchette very lightly" I commanded

Everyone looked at each other nervously, questioning with their eyes, who's going to do it first?!
No one moved.

"Ok, I'll do it first, you'll see nothing is going to happen" William offered to do it first. His hands were trembling as he moved towards the planchette, slowly.
William is a close friend of mine since middle school. We met in the 7th grade and ever since then we've been inseparable.

"Is anybody there?" William asked the board.
Nothing . .

"Is anybody there?!" He asked again ..
We heard a small rumbling coming from the ceiling above us.
We looked around, startled. The ceiling rumbled again. The planchet began to move under William's fingertips.
"Ohhh what the hell?!"
The planchet moved to "yes".

Then everything went dark, so cliché' but it happened.
"No one move" I said

We all held hands, frozen with fright. What the heck was going on?
The rumbling that was once coming from the ceiling was nice right under us. It shook the table where the board was. The table started to shake violently. We all screamed and the table stopped moving. The board and the planchette stood right in the middle of the table as if never touched.

"WHAT IS GOING ON HERE?!!" The owner of the botanica we were in scared the lights out of us .

"Uhhhh... ummmmm.. we could explain !!!!" Rebeca said
"Ok, explain!!" she said
"Well.. ummm... we were just curious as to what this was .. that's all" i responded

"You have no idea what you just did here, No idea" the lady said back

"You just opened up a dangerous portal and made something come out, something that was meant to stay dormant forever"

"What was meant to stay dormant? What came out of the portal?" Diana asked afraid

"Come, follow me and I'll show you"

We all grabbed our belongings and followed the lady out of the corridor we were in and into a small room in the store.

"What if she's trying to kidnap us?"
"Rebeca, shut up" I said shaking my head.

The room we went into was the size of a walk in closet in a mansion. One of those with like a million shoes in them .. but it was kind of dark, the lights were low, gave it a mellow ambience. There were also books, lots of books. Stephen King, Dean Koontz, Anne Rice

and other authors. There were also books I've have never ever seen before. No author names printed on them but the titles seems like if they were written in Latin.

The lady, which by the way her name was Abigail, pulled out a book from a shelf from the backend corner of the room. It was a big black book, old looking and dusty. She started to flip through the pages and stopped at a specific page. She stared at it for awhile before she began to talk.

"You see this here?" She asked us, pointing at a horrific picture of a creature of some sort. "This.. this thing, this is what you just unleashed from the board. It goes by the name of Zozo. He is the Ouija board demon."

"Ouija board demon?, seriously?" Diana asked in disbelief.

"Yea, seriously".. she looked at all of us with a serious look of concern, it creeped me out.

"You guys don't know what you're messing with" she stated

"If this thing... "Zozo" as you call it, is so bad, then why did you have the board to begin with?"

Abigail looked at all of us blankly..

" That's none of your concern" she stated
"My question to you is, why were you snooping

around to begin with?"

"I was just curious, that's all" I explained

"Well you being nosey got you and your friends into some trouble. I hope you all sleep well tonight" Abigail stated

"Whatever man, let's just go, this is bugging me out" Rebeca expressed

We all walked out of the Botanica a bit shaken up. We were all silent on our walk home. I was thinking to myself to come back tomorrow and ask Abigail more questions about this demon she seems afraid of. Im curious about it now.

The next day..

"Jen, are you out of your damn mind? Didn't that lady make it clear to you already?" Rebeca yelled.

"I know she made it clear but I just need to know why it exist and why she was using the board. Was she trying to contact that demon herself or what? I need to know."

"You don't work for the Scooby-Doo Detective Agency, you don't need to know a damn thing. Stay away from the Botanica before you get yourself into some shit you'll regret" Rebeca always gave me a damn lecture. I hated it, she was always right but I never listened.

I went home and did some research on this so called demon.
This demon is in fact the Ouija board demon.
It was the scariest looking thing I have seen!!!
It is said that this demon is the destroyer of souls and also changes lives. How can something that can't be seen destroy a soul?

Now I'm even more curious to know more about it.
I might have to use the Ouija board for that.
Rebeca is seriously going to kill me.

Part 3

"What the hell is wrong with you Jen?!" all my friends yelled at me.

"Are you seriously telling me that you actually believe that this 'demon" is real? I asked

We were all standing in front of the botanica chatting about my "brilliant idea". Well not chatting, more like me getting yelled at like if I was a child. I wanted to go in the botanica and buy a Ouija board, my friends obviously weren't up for that idea.

"C'mon guys, let me get it and try it out. I'll prove to you that Zozo isn't real."
As I said those words a man dressed in all white, white head scarf, white beads, shirt and pants walked by me and stopped dead in his tracks. He looked like a Santero. A Santero is a priest of a religious cult like a witch doctor maybe or maybe not.

"He is evil, he's nothing to be played with at least not on your own" the man stated

"Uuummm ok, thanks" I responded

"I'm serious, you can get yourself and your friends in a lot of danger if you call upon THAT demon who's name shouldn't even be pronounced" the man said.

We all looked at him like if he was crazy. "Bro, who the hell are you?" Diana asked who was nonchalantly eating an ice cream cone.

"My name is Ruiz"
"What type of name is Ruiz?" Rebeca asked sarcastically
"It's my last name sweetie, my friends call me by my first name, clearly you aren't friends" he responded with a smirk.

Rebeca rolled her eyes at the man.

"So how evil is this Zo..'
"Shhhhhhh... do not mention his name. That's like tempting him to come to you. Its like calling Bloody Mary or Slender man or some weird creature from the unknown" Ruiz whispered

"What the hell is a Slender man?" Diana asked
"That's a whole different story for another day, follow me I might be able to help you" Ruiz commanded.

Diana, William, Rebeca and I followed Ruiz into this alley that lead to a basement behind a grocery store. I thought it was going to be dark and damp but it was actually brightly lit and smelled like strawberry candles.
I scanned the place just to see if I saw anything strange. I did. I found what I was looking for. I found an altar.
Santeros always have one of those in their homes. It's a table full of candles and saints that they pray to everyday like the one my grandma and God mother had.

He had a big white couch and a nice fur carpet in the middle of his room. He asked us to sit and that he will be right back. He disappeared and Diana looked at me like if I was crazy.

"Why are we here?!! What if he's trying to kill us?!!!"

"I'm not trying to kill you" he walked back into the room with something in his hand. It was a Ouija Board.

He sat in the middle of the rug. "Please take off your shoes and join me in a circle"

I stepped up first. I was anxious to see what was his plan. The rest of my friends followed me. We took off our shoes and sat criss crossed apple sauce style.

"What do you plan on doing Ruiz?" William asked nervously

"I'm going to show you that this thing you want to contact is indeed real. We're going to contact it" Ruiz stated

"We sounds like a lot of people, I ain't doing shit, I'm out of here" Rebeca was getting u from the circle until I grabbed her arm and pulled her back down.

"You're staying"

She grilled me. "You're making a huge mistake and I guarantee you that something will go wrong"

Ruiz wiped the board off with a white cloth and set a cold glass of water next to it. We all held hands, bowed our heads and said a prayer before we began. My palms were sweaty. I was scared shitless but I was curious to find out what this thing really was. If it was really real or something made up by Abigail so we didn't bother her anymore.

We were all silent.

"We wish to commune with the Ouija board spirit, are you amongst us?" Ruiz began "Please show us a sign that you are here"

Silence.

We heard a low rumble, as if someone rolled a bowling ball on the floor and then a door slammed shut.

"What the..?" Diana whispered

"It's here" Ruiz said with a seriously deep tone in his voice

We all turned to look at him. His eyes, they weren't his eyes anymore, they were black, completely black. The darkest eyes I have ever seen. He look at all of us and gave us the most grotesque grin. Razor sharp yellow teeth. His skin, his skin had changed. His face was scarred with scratches and boils. His piercing black eyes watched us like a wolf watches its prey. We all started to back away scared out of our minds. Ruiz or whatever he was stood up from the floor and over towered us. His breathing was heavy and raspy. His grin was wider, he was drooling. He looked so evil. Something definitely went wrong.

"I TOLD YOU, I FUCKING TOLD YOU, YOU NEVER LISTEN TO ME" Rebeca yelled at me.
Ruiz levitated off the floor. His place became very cold and very windy and loud.

"Oh my God, what the fuck is going ooooonnnn??!!" William was screaming over the wind and loud, monstrous moans.

"I don't know"" I yelled back " but we need to get out of here NOOOWWWW"

We all got up and started to run to the door but we were stopped by some sort of pressure. We couldn't move.

"You're not going anywhere. You wanted Zozo, here I am"

We all screamed in unison. Next thing I knew I hear William scream in so much pain. I see him struggling in the air, trying to fight whatever is holding him up. He's kicking and screaming and then.. CRACK! His spine is snapped and he's split in half from the torso. William is gone.
I couldn't make a sound. My voice was stuck in my throat.

"OH MY GOD, OH MY GOOODDDD!!!!!!" Diana screamed hysterically

All while this is going on, Ruiz is in the middle of the room, floating in the air looking at us laughing his evil laugh. His arms outstretched taking in the scenery in his living room.

"Ruiz stop all of this" Rebeca demanded

"Ruiz doesn't live here anymore, never did... "

Ruiz was the demon all along. He tricked us. I should of listened to my friends, I should of.

More screaming. Diana was sliding across the floor.

"HEEELLLPPPP"

I tried grabbing her foot but couldn't read her on time. Her head slammed so hard on the wall that it cracked her skull open. Oh Jesus, so much blood.

It was just Rebeca and I now. We held on to each other.

"Rebby, I'm so sorry.. I'm truly sorry" I cried
"It's to late for that Jenny, we have to get out of here, we have to try"

In that instant Rebeca held her stomach tight.
"It's burning, aaahhhhhh. it burns'

Zozo or Ruiz, I don't know anymore, was scratching and burning her stomach.

"STOP!! STOP IT!!" I yelled at it

"JENNYYYYYY!!!!!!" She scream.

BOOM!! The apartment door slammed open. It was Abigail, the lady from the botanica. She ran in threw some sort of liquid at Zozo. It made a horrible, terrifying noise. It pulled its head back in pain and then growled at Abigail.

"You're mine" It said

"Girls go, get out while you can, I'll handle this bitch" Abigail insisted

"GOOOOO" She yelled

We ran out of the apartment and into the alley. We were panting, out of breath. A huge cloud covered the building we were by. Loud thunder rolled over the building and lighting struck a tree near by. And then a large roar over our heads, we look up and see black smoke rise above and into the cloud. The cloud then disappeared, vanished as if it was never there.

"What the hell?" we both whispered

"What the hell is right, I told you that you unleased something powerful" Abigail walked out of the apartment wiping off her clothes.

We looked at her wide eyed. Glad that she was ok.

"You don't have to worry about him for awhile. I released the dark souls that kept him alive and *burp*, excuse me" she said while wiping her mouth

"I also ate his heart, taste a little burnt but it'll do for now, but a word of advice, please don't mess with the Ouija board again"

"Yes ma'am" We told her still looking confused as to what the hell just happened

I never played with that shit again...
'

Don't Fall Asleep

There have been a lot of stories about the dark web. I didn't believe any of them were true. That is until I found this lap top at an internet café. Now I think my life is in danger.

Why is my life in danger you ask? Let me explain. I walked into a 24 hour café late last night, ordered a latte and sat across another table. On the table across from me sat an Acer gaming lap top. It was opened with no one around it. I asked the barista if it was hers and she said no. I walked over to it and sat, as soon as I saw the screen turned on. I saw a room, an empty room with a chair in front of the what I assumed was the lap top camera.

"Hello?" I spoke into the laptop.
Nothing!

I decided to type instead..
"Hello, is anyone there?" maybe they can hear the notification sound.

"NOOOOOOOO, GET AWAAAAYYYY"
A girl ran onto the screen screaming frantically.

"Oh my God" she whimpered
"Now it's going to come for you too"

"Who's coming for me?" I asked.. confused

"You wont be able to see it but you'll know it's there" The girl cried on to the screen. Then she started to look around her room, frightened.

"It's coming back, I can feel it" then she disappears from the screen. She ran off somewhere. I look around the coffee shop, it's empty. I'm all alone.

"Excuse me!" I yelled "Miss, are you here?"

No answer...

Then I heard a blood curling scream coming from the lap top. The girl, she was... floating in midair. Levitated off the floor by something unseen.

"What the…?
She was kept in the air for a moment then dropped hard to the floor.

"Oh my God" I gasped
The barista came out from where she was and asked if I was ok.

"I just seen something on the screen.
I turned to face the laptop and it was off. I began to press the keyboard to wake it back up, pressed the on and off button and nothing seemed to work. It seemed like it was dead.

"I swear it was just.. AHHHH GET AWAY FROM ME, STOP!"
As I turned around to continue speaking to the barista I saw the most repulsive face I have ever seen in my life. It was twisted, malformed. It's eyes were white, its teeth were rotten, smelled like …like.. oh the smell was death. It turned my stomach.
I ran but before running out the door it grabbed me and put its face to mine, so close that I can see the rotting skin bleed. It said something to me.

"Don't go to sleep" it whispered in a very raspy and creepy voice.
I closed my eyes so tight and asked it.. "Whhhy?" with a stutter.
All I heard was a maniacal laugh. I screamed as it laughed and teased me. I wept until I felt "it" let go. I opened my eyes and "it" was gone.

I ran home and haven't left my house ever since. Its been two weeks now, I'm running out of food. I did some research and found out that what I was watching that night at the coffee shop came from the dark net and there's supposedly an evil spirit haunting the net. It found me and its trying to get me. I keep hearing strange noises in my home. I haven't slept either but my eyes are getting really heavy now...

"Don't fall asleep"... a distant whisper in the dark..

It Came From The Woods

Harold and I were sitting on his front porch talking and having a few drinks and some pizza. "You ever wondered what's in the woods? He randomly asked me.

"What do you mean?" I asked while stuffing a slice of pizza in my mouth.

"I mean, do you ever wonder what's in there? They don't allow anyone to go in there anymore because of some disappearance that happened like two years ago with some kid" he responded while chewing like a cow

"Oh, I heard about that situation. I've heard about a whole bunch of shit that has happened. That kid that you're talking about, he was dared to go into the woods. He used to hang out with a group of bad ass kids and of course he was one of them too but he was the youngest one so they picked on him a lot. Anyways, they wanted to prove how tough he really was so they dared him to go into the woods alone, find the cabin that's by the creek and stay there until sunrise and walk back. Him being the dumb kid that he was, just to show off he agreed to it but deep inside he was scared shitless.

Stupid mistake on his part..

"What the hell happened?" Harold interrogated

"Shut up let me finish!" I exclaimed

"So that night they sneaked out of their windows walked the kid to the clearing of the woods at around midnight. They gave h'm a book bag with food and a flashlight and sent him on his way. He hesitated to walk in but they pushed him in and he fell. They told him to get up before he got beat up by them. He got up and ran into the woods."

"That's messed up man" Harold seemed upset.

"Wait, it gets worst" I responded
"He ran into the woods afraid of his so called friends. As he walked he turned on his flashlight. His "friends" saw the flashlight shinning and waited until he got deeper into the woods so they can go in and scare him. This is when it starts to get scary. Supposedly the kid was deep in the woods and found the cabin. He ran inside the cabin because he was hearing strange noises. Of course we will think it was his friends making the noises right? .. Wrong! His friends were still by the clearing trying to figure out a

plan to scare him. The kid busted through the door and slammed it behind him. He was panting heavily. He took a peek out one of the windows and didn't see anything but he still heard the noises surrounding the house.

He ran up the stairs in the cabin and hid in a closet in one of the bedrooms. He was petrified, all alone and hungry. Suddenly he heard something coming up the stairs. The stairs were creaking as if whatever was coming up the stairs was taunting him, letting him know it was coming for him. Then the footsteps stopped right in front of the bedroom door. He heard the door slowly opening. The kid was sweating profusely. He wanted to scream, wanted to cry but knew he couldn't.

It continued to walk into the room. The kid was paralyzed with fear.
It walked up to the closet door and jiggled the door knob. It knew the kid was in there. It probably smelled him since he basically pissed himself from the fear.

The jiggling stopped then the door forcefully swung open. He screamed but saw nothing. The kid scanned the room from inside the open door. "Hello" he whispered.

"HELLO" a disembodied voice replied back. Something grabbed him and he screamed a blood curling scream that was heard through the woods.

His friends heard the scream, looked at one another and all ran towards the cabin. When they got closer to the cabin they stopped about ten feet away and just stared.

"Wait, they actually had the balls to go that far?" Harold asked.

"I mean yeah, if I had heard your screams coming from somewhere that I clearly know its forbidden to go to, I'll go to rescue you" I responded

"You better!" Harold said while shoving another slice of pizza in his mouth.

"Alright shut up, let me finish. So they all stared at the cabin. The toughest dude walked up to the house, you know there's always a tough guy in the group, and yelled out the kid's name, no answer. He stepped on to the porch, they all followed behind him. They walked into the cabin and it was pitch black and dusty. Guess no one has been there in awhile. One of the guys asked, "Isn't this place supposed to be haunted?"

"Seriously?! Haunted?!, I doubt it. Abandoned yes, haunted? I don't think so" The tough responded back.

BANG! They heard a door upstairs slam closed. They all jumped startled at the same.
"It was just the wind" the guy said.

"Suuuure, the wind" the other kid said

They headed up the stairs vey slowly. It was even darker upstairs. They tried to adjust their vision and kept moving around. They opened different doors one at a time. The rooms were partially empty. A few beds, chairs and a lot of dust.

They reached the last door.

"He's got to be in here, if he's not then we're out, he'll eventually appear. This place gives me the creeps" one of the guys expressed.

"Man shut up, you're such a punk" the tough guy teased.

"Bro, something isn't right here, their aren't any windows open up here so the wind couldn't possibly shut the door"
As soon as the scared kid said his last words the door in front of them slowly opened. The kid was standing in the room in front of a closed window.

They whispered his name. "Jose".. no response. "Jose!" they said a little louder this time, still nothing.

Of course the big tough guy wanted to be all mean as usual so he walked into the room and grabbed Jose's right shoulder.
"Bro , stop playing around man, lets go!"

Jose wouldn't move. The tough guy slowly moved his hand away from Jose's shoulder.
"He's freezing, he feels like a dead corpse" the kid said

The room began to feel cold too, they could see cold smoke breath coming out their mouths.

"Jose come on man lets go, lets get out of here"
one of the other guys said.

Jose turned around and with the most creepiest
voice that can come out of a human's mouth
he said, "We're not going anywhere"

His eyes, they were completely bloodshot white.
He looked so evil, his smile was sinister. The guys
started to walk backwards out of the room as
Jose walked closer to them. They turned around
and ran except for the tough guy who tried to
run but fell to the floor. Jose picked him up by
levitating him. The guy was floating in the air,
screaming for dear life. The other guys had ran
out the house, heard the scream and continued
to run.

Jose and the guy were never to be seen again.

"Wow, what the ...?!" the expression on Harold's
face was priceless.
"Yup" I said

"That's insane. I didn't know those woods were
haunted. Has anything else ever happened after
that? "Harold asked

"I've heard about two dumb girls who went in there to play the Ouija board but that's it. Heard they got a real good scare, ha ha" I told him while I took a sip of my drink.

"I don't know" Harold seemed skeptical.
"I don't believe things until I see it for myself" he said.

"What is it that you want to see?" I asked him

"The cabin. I want to go inside and see what we find"

They both sat there, quiet..

"Wait!" he shouted
I looked at him perplexed.
"How the hell do you know this story? Were you there? Did you see what happened? He insisted an answer.
I sat there.. playing with my fingers.
"Yea... I was there" I told him
"Whaaaatttt???!!!, what you mean you were there? He was shocked and a bit upset.
"You kept this a secret for so long, why? He asked me

Silence…

"Hellooo!!!"

I looked up at him and he pushed himself back, startled.
"What the fuck?" he whispered

My eyes were bloodshot white, my smirk was evil, malevolent. The voice that came out of me was disembodied, inhumane.

"Because… I'm Jose!"

Doors

I have a fear when it comes to open doors.
Any open door that isn't supposed to be open terrifies me, gives me the creeps, it just scares the hell out of me. I walk around my apartment closing every door I see open, even the bathroom door.
There's has been times when I've gone to bed, all doors closed and I have woken up scared.

One night I felt weird, like if someone was in the room with me. I felt a heavy presence. I have two closets in my room and one of the doors was open, wide open. My eyes weren't adjusted just yet to the dark but I knew something was there. I didn't dare get off my bed but eventually had to so I can shut the door and go back to sleep.

I waited a few minutes and got up. As I got up I felt the room get colder than the usual. "Fuck" I whispered to myself.
I knew exactly what that meant, there was a spirit in the room. Yea I'm very into the paranormal so I know the feeling of having a presence around. This wasn't a good feeling.

As I approached the closet it got colder, so cold that I could see my own breath in the dark.
"Jesus Christ" I whispered again. Whatever was in the room growled at me right after I said the name of Christ. I just stirred something up. I backed up the my bed and woke up my husband.

"Babe?!" i quietly said.
"Hmmm" he mumbled

"The closet door is open again. I think there's something here with us"
My husband knows I'm afraid and doesn't judge me. What?! You thought I was going to say he's

like the typical husband and he's a skeptic?
Nope, he's not like that!

He got up and picked up the bat that he keeps
besides his bedside and walked slowly towards
the closet. He felt the cold and stopped
midway.

"Jesus Christ" he then heard the growl too.
"Oh shit" I said.
I'm turning on my phone flashlight" I told him
"Ok"
I reached for my phone and turned the flashlight
on in the direction of the closet. I instantly regret
that. What we saw was the most hideous face
we have ever seen. We screamed as it
screamed a monstrous, terrifying sound.
My husband ran past it and turned the room
light on. It was gone. I came up from the side of
my bed and saw that nothing was there.

"What the hell?"

"I don't know babe but pack your shit, we're
going to a hotel" my husband demanded.

We rushed and packed a few things and left. Left all the lights on. The rest of the night was peaceful.

The following day I went to speak to the landlord and broke the lease. We weren't planning and coming back. I went into the apartment to get the rest of our belongings. As I was packing a few more things to take with me, I felt extremely uncomfortable being there.
It was watching me. I know it was. I felt it.

I turned around and saw the closet door open. It was closed when I came in, I'm pretty sure of it. I rushed to get my belongings. I walked towards the bedroom door to leave and it slammed shut.

"LEAVE ME ALONE, JUST LET ME BE" I yelled at absolutely nothing.
I sunk myself onto the floor and cried. Suddenly I felt a cold gust of wind. Something was standing in front of me, I could smell it.
It grabbed me by the neck, pushed me up against the wall. I couldn't breathe.
it lifted me off the floor. I tried to scream but just choking sounds only came out.

I heard footsteps approaching the room. The door swung open. It was the landlord. As soon as he opened the door and looked at me, whatever it was that had me by the neck let go of me and dropped me. The landlord helped me up and we ran out of the apartment.

I called and told my husband what had just happened.

We never went back to that apartment, we left everything we owned there and started brand new. Now we live in a beautiful Victorian house in Sleepy Hollow, Long Island. The house if pretty old so it makes a lot of noise when it settles at night and there's this horrific smell, I think it's coming from the attic. I think IT followed us here. I'm very afraid to find out.

The Warehouse

"You think this is a good idea?" Julio asked
"I don't think it is but I'm daring" I said it with a
smirk on my face.
"I heard it was haunted, why not go check if its
true?"

It was an old abandoned warehouse in the
middle of nowhere on Hunts Point. It was located

at the end of a desolate street where auto parts were sold during the day. It was huge. It was a complete mess to put it nicely. From the outside, the boarded windows and door that was bolted with iron rods, all looked scary and threatening enough to keep us away. I'm pretty sure behind the closed door it was much worst and I couldn't wait to go inside.

It was five of us tonight, on this dreadful day of the dead, good ol' O' hallows eve, Halloween night!

Julio who was my best friend was down for whatever. He's a skeptic though but he supports my crazy.

Yari is my sister, we're so much alike in so many ways. We've experienced so much growing up together and going into this adventure has us ecstatic.

Jessica is another great friend of mine. She was such a sweetheart and she kept it real with me all the time.

"Girl, are you sure about this?" Jessica questioned me

"Are you going to chicken out now?" I questioned her back

"No, but I'm just asking cause this doesn't look safe"

"We'll be fine, I brought some masks to help us breath incase there's asbestos or whatever"

There's one more person missing and I'm getting impatient waiting for him but nervous at the same time. Then off into the distance I saw someone walking towards us. He was wearing a black t-shirt and a black snap back with grey sweatpants. I started to tremble. My hands were sweaty.

"Who's that?" my sister asked
"That right there... that's Noel" Jessica smirked
"Oooooohhhhhh" Yari giggled
He approached us, the girls waved at him and he waved back. He said whats up to Julio and gave him a pound.
He came closer to me...
"Hi Jen" he whispered
"Hey" I shyly greeted him

He got a bit closer and gave me a hug. I smelled his sweet cologne scent. It was amazing. He smelled like .. Downy and cologne. Ok I have to snap out of it.

Everyone was staring. I broke away.
"OK! Let's go inside" I said out loud.
Noel smiled.

We all walked to the door of the warehouse.

"Did you bring the crowbar like I asked you to? I asked Noel.
"Yeah its right here" he showed it to me and then stuck it to a piece of wood on the door and began to remove the two by fours.

We were finally inside. This place was surrounded by dust and cobwebs. Julio pulled out a flashlight from his book bag and turned it on. They began to walk in further into the warehouse. There were sheets on furniture, broken tables and chairs. The paint was peeling off, there were holes on the wooden floors and off in the distance was a gloomy staircase.

"BINGO!" I excitedly squealed
"Let's start upstairs"

"What exactly are we looking for?" Julio stopped dead in his tracks

"This place is supposed to be haunted" I paused "So let's go find whatever haunts this place and why"

A loud scream was heard coming from behind where I stood. Something pushed me, hard. I tripped over something on the floor, fell and hit my head. I was instantly knocked out.

*She walked into the abandoned building, looked and saw nothing but darkness. She continued walking into the dark corridor. It was damp, muggy. She walked into some spider webs and screamed, "Oh Jesus Christ".

She heard her echo down the long corridor and scared herself. Suddenly she felt a cold chill in front of her, so cold that she noticed a breath of smoke but it wasn't her breathe. Seemed like something was standing in front of her.

"Who's there?" she asked
No response… but then something happened, she felt a hand touch her on her back.

"Ouch" she felt a burning feeling

She turned around and saw nothing, no one was there.

"This is insane. I need to get out here" she told herself

But something told her to keep walking deeper into the building. It kept getting darker the more she walked in. She heard a whisper coming from behind her. When she turned to look she saw a figure, a distorted figure.

"Jen wake up, please wake up" Yari cried

I moved around, rubbed my head, tried to get to get back up but immediately laid back down. I was way to dizzy.

"Oh God" I mumbled. "What happened?"

"You fell babe, it looked like you were pushed and hit the floor hard" Noel explained while holding me.

When I realized he was holding me I tried getting back up but he held me back.

"Chill, stop trying to move" he demanded

"I'm fine!" I exclaimed but stood in place

"I had a dream, a vision or whatever.., it was weird. I saw a girl walking in a dark building, looked just like this one but it felt like she wasn't alone"

My friends suspiciously all looked at each other..

"Ummm" Jessica seem hesitant

"We saw something while you were knocked out that scared the shit out of us, it wasn't human and it wasn't friendly"

"Whaa.. what are you talking about?, what was it? What did you see?" I rushed my questions, I was panicking.

"It was a girl" Julio went on.

"Well at least that's what it looked like. She looked disproportioned, scary"

He shivered.

"Her clothes were torn, she wore the typical white dress but it was so dirty and it had what looked like dried up blood spots all over. Her hair was long, black and filthy. There was some sort of mist surrounding her, more like fog. Her held a ragged doll in her hand, looked like that raggedy Anne doll. Her eyes, they were as bright as the moonlight" Julio was lost in his words.

"She spoke" Yari intervened.

"What did she say?" I asked still being held by Noel.

"You're mine"

"What the hell does she mean by that?" I asked confused but continued

"Shit, I definitely don't belong to her, she better cut that out"

"Well I don't know but we need to get out of here before she comes back and we actually find out" Julio was saying while trying to help me get off the floor and off Noel.

"My man, what are you doing?" Noel asked Julio

"What does is look like I'm doing?, I'm trying to help her up, we gotta go" Julio sneered at Noel

Noel smacked Julio's hand off my arm. "I got her".

Julio gave him an evil look and let go of my arm.

"This isn't the time for this, I'm good" I told them both while getting myself off the floor and wiping the dust away.

"Thank you" I told Noel, shyly looked at him and smiled.

"I don't know what's going on with me but I gotta chill" I thought to myself.

"So what are we going to do now" Jessica asked.

For a moment I felt a cold chill on the back of my neck. I shivered. It became really cold really fast.

"Do you guy's feel that?" I asked

"Yeah" Yari was giving herself a bear hug, rubbing her arms to keep warm.

"That means one thing, that thing is coming back."

We all started walking towards the exit but stopped dead in our tracks. By the exit was a black looking figure. It had no shape, it looked more like some sort of smoke just floating, blocking the doorway.

"What in theeee…." Jessica whispered..

The black smoke expanded, it became larger and began to spread all around us. We had no way out. The warehouse became much darker, wind came out of nowhere, everything was flying everywhere and it made it hard to see. It felt like a tornado.

"What the hell is going on?, What are we going to do?" Yari yelled over the loud wind.

"We have to figure a way to run through the smoke and find the exit" Julio yelled.

We started looking around but saw nowhere to go, we were stuck.

"I have an idea" I yelled

I always walked around with a small cross around my neck, it's something my best friend made me wear everyday since the day we had a horrible experience with a Ouija Board.

I pulled out the cross from my neck and began to shout the prayer from The Exorcist, it was the only prayer I knew.

"The Power Of Christ Compels You"

I began to chant. As I kept going everyone else joined in.

"The power of Christ compels you, the power of Christ compels you"

The wind began to slow down, it was working.

We chanted louder and louder.. the wind stopped.

Silence!

Our eyes moved around the warehouse. Nothing.

"Come on lets go" I spotted a window on the side behind some old boxes.

"Noel can you use your crowbar to move that plank? He moved towards the window and climbed a box to get closer to it.

He began to remove the wood off the windows when he suddenly flew a few feet away and slammed up against a wall and fell to the ground.

"Oh My GOD" I yelled an I ran to him.

The floor began to tremble uncontrollably making it hard to get to Noel. I stumbled but made my way towards hi.

"Are you ok?" I shouted over the rumbling noise.

"Yeah I'm fine. Let's get out of here"

"YOU'RE NOT GOING ANYWHERE!!!"

Something screamed from behind us. It was that thing, that girl that I must have dreamt about when I was unconscious. She was floating above us, she looked... terrifyingly angry, enraged. She looked like a demon.

She swooped down towards us and smacked Julio on the face so hard she made him fall to the dusty old floor where he landed on a sharp object and it penetrated his leg.

"AAAAHHHHHHH What the....!!!!!" He screamed in agony.

"Somebody HELP MEEE"

We ran to check on him. The girl came back and tried attacking one of us but we all ducked away from her. She missed. We checked on

Julio, tried to help up. While we helped him, Yari ran a different direction.

"Guy's I have a plan, I saw something I can use to against this bitch."

Yari picked up a metal bat she saw in the distance, probably something left behind some teen and his friends.

"Next time she comes down I'm swinging, I heard metal hurts spirits" Yari exclaimed, looking determined to hurt that thing.

"WATCH IT!" Jess yelled.

She was coming back down towards us, we all duct down except Yari. She cocked her arms back and swung at the spirit, hard. The bat went right through the girl and made her disappear.

"Good shit Yari!!" Julio yelled

"Let's goooo" Noel had already opened the door for us to get out. We helped Julio up and ran as fast as we could out the door and slammed it shut behind us before she came back.

We all stopped to catch our breathes, turned back around and looked at the warehouse. She was standing by a widow on the second floor. She screamed so loud that It shattered the remaining windows that were damaged from the building being abandoned.

We all ran and never looked back.

A Personal Experience #1

Since I've been sharing stories that I've made up on my own, I've decided to share some personal experiences. One of the reasons as to why I love horror and the paranormal so much is because of what I've experienced. Its always something strange. I've never been afraid of spirits. People think I'm crazy when I talk about them but I don't really care. I'm not afraid, I have definitely felt them around me, I caught glimpse of strange things but then again.. who hasn't?

I remember one night, it was about maybe 4 a.m. I had woken up because I guess I just felt strange. When I opened my eyes I saw Emma, my daughter for those who don't know, sitting up on her bed. During this time she was around maybe 4 or 5 years old. She was sitting in the middle of her bed staring into darkness, staring into one of the corners of our bedroom. I looked at the corner after putting on my glasses, yea I'm nearly blind without them, and saw nothing.

I asked Emma if she was ok and she didn't respond. Then she got up and climbed into my bed and sat between her dad and I but kept focus on the corner. She was holding her favorite blanket which she still has till this day, she was holding it tight. My vision finally adjusted to the dark and then I finally saw what she was looking at. It was a tall, dark figure. I saw its reflection through the mirror. It slightly move, that's how I noticed it.

I grabbed Emma and laid her down next to me. I held her tight and prayed for awhile until I fell asleep with her in my arms. The next morning we woke up and Emma didn't remember a thing...

Fear

You've ever had that feeling when you turn off the living room lights and begin to walk back to your room. You have this uneasy feeling that there's someone or something behind you...

Be careful.. don't look back..!

A Personal Experience #2

One summer morning, it was about 6 a.m. my honey and I were sleeping. I randomly woke up because I felt the sheets being pulled off of me. We had a quilt on the bed because our air conditioner is amazing. Any who, I opened my eyes and actually saw the quilt being pulled off. I was slowly sliding off the bed. I thought I was dreaming so I pulled the sheet back up, turned over and fell back asleep. What felt like forever was literary 10 minutes when I woke back up because the sheets once again were being pulled. This time my hubby woke up and felt it too. He asked me to stop and I said it wasn't me that was doing it.

He finally looked at the quilt, looked at me and was shocked at what he saw. We both pulled the quilt back up at the same time. He got up to check because I definitely wasn't doing so (I was actually freaked out) and checked if it was our cat playing around.

It wasn't. We don't have an under bed because our bed frame is wooden and it reaches the floor so nothing can go underneath it. So there was nothing there pulling the quilt. We didn't sleep after that.

Dark

You wake up to the soft sound of scratching on your bedroom.

The door slowly opens but you cant see a thing because its to dark. You hear a whisper coming from the left side of you. You cover your head with your blanket and wait a little while. While your eyes are still closed you slowly move the blanket off your face and just listen.

Nothing!

But then you feel something wet drip on your forehead.

Drip.. drip.. drip..

You open your eyes and see the most terrifying, pale, grotesque, haunting face right above you. It's smiling at you, that's the last thing you see before it muffles your screams!

<u>It Knocked Twice</u>

(A Snapchat Story)

Late one evening, I was home alone doing what I do best, Snap chatting!

Opens Snapchat

Snapping Jamil

Me – "Heeeeey Boo!"

Closes Snapchat

While I wait on my homie Jamil to respond I go to the kitchen and open the fridge.

"What the hell am I going to eat?" I asked myself.

"Ha!" I exclaimed when I saw the leftover ground beef.

"Tacos it is for tonight"

I took a bowl, slipped it into the microwave and heated it up.

Ding

The snapchat notification went off.

Opens Snapchat

Opens Message

J – " Wassup love? Wyd?"

I snapped a picture of the microwave.

Me – " Heating up something to eat, im staving"

Sent

The microwaves beeps. I begin to prepare my meal and another message came in.

Opens Snapchat

Opens message

J – "What are we eating?"

Me – "WE sounds like a lot of people. I'M about to eat tacos though"

J – "Wooooord! That sounds good right now. Send me a pic."

Me - *Pic sent*

J – "Oh hell yea, I'm coming over ha ha. Send me a pic of yourself"

Me – "Why?"

J – "Because… I want to see your pretty face"

Blushing, I smiled.

Pic sent

Jamil Opens Pic

J – "you look beautiful…, is there someone at home with you?"

I looked at my phone.

"Here we go again." I thought to myself

Me – "No Jamil, I'm home alone, everyone is out for the night"

J – "So who's that standing behind you? Looks like they're in the living room"

I turned around to face the living room but nothing or anyone was there.

"What the hell is he talking about?" I asked myself

Opens Snapchat

Me – "Bro, what the hell are you talking about? There's no one

here."

J – "I swear there was someone there. I'm gonna edit the picture and show you"

Me – "Please do cause if this is how you think you're coming over, it's not working"

While I waited for his response I walked to my room and sat on my bed with my tacos and drink and put on a movie.

The notification went off again.

Open Snapchat

"Oh shit! What the fuck?!" I yelled in disbelief, covered my mouth right after. I was stuck on what I saw. It was a tall dark figure, I couldn't see it's face, it was distorted.

Me – "Did you photo shop that figure in there? Are you trying to scare me?"

J – "Hell no! I'm not trying to scare you, on the contrary, that shit scared me, just thought I'd warn you."

Me - "Well there's no one here, so I'm gonna watch a movie and eat, I'll hit you up later.

J – "Alright love ttyl"

I put my phone down and started to watch some paranormal movie, as a matter of fact it was Grave Encounters, one of my all time favorites.

"Crap, I left my drinky drink" I got up and walked over to the kitchen to retrieve my drink when I got startled.

Knock, knock

I stopped and looked at my apartment door. *Who could that be? I thought to myself*

"Who is it?" I shouted

No response.. I looked through the peep hole, no one there.

"Hmm, probably wrong door"

I took my drink and walked back to my room. The atmosphere felt a little different but I didn't really pay any mind to it.

"Oouuu I can't wait to eat these tacos!"

I pressed play on the movie. I was about to take my first bite of those delicious cheesy tacos when..

Knock, knock

It sounded faint, a light knocking. I picked up my phone.

Opens snapchat

Me – "JAMIL, ARE YOU KNOCKING ON MY DOOR?!!!"

He quickly responded..

J – "Ummm no, I don't even know where you live. Why?"

Me – "Well there's someone knocking on my door, at least I think its coming from the door. It's the second time it happens. I checked the first time and no one was there. I thought it may be you playing around."

J – "It's definitely not me but if you want I can go and keep you company."

Me – "Nah, I think I'll be ok"

J – "You sure?, I'm not convinced but you let me know if you change your mind"

Me – "Thanks, I'll keep you posted"

"I must be buggin' out" I thought to myself again

Part 2

I went back to my movie. The next hour was quiet and the movie had gotten intense.

Suddenly my bedroom door slammed shut.

"Oh heeeellllll no" I said as I reached for my phone.

Opens Snapchat

*Send Voice note"

Me – "Jamil, now I need you to come, my bedroom door just slammed shut, I'm pinning you my address right now, I don't want to be alone"

Voice note from Jamil

J – "What you mean your door slammed shut? Maybe a open window?"

Send voice note

Me – "NO! my window's are closed, I'll show you"

*Record video"

Me – (Video) "Look my windows are closed and look at my door, closed and...I know you see that, look at the door knob, it's moving"

I shrieked, moving back away from the door.

Video call

J – "Yo what the hell???!!!"

The door knob stopped moving.

Knock, knock

Me – (I was in tears) "Bro, there's someone in my house, they're knocking on the door. Please tell me you hear that'"

Jamil is looking at me from the phone trying to figure out to do.

Me – "Should I open the door and see who it is?"

J - " Are you crazy? That's so cliché, you know you shouldn't open the door dummy, I'm on my way, stay put"

Me – " How long until you get here?"

"AHHHHHHHHH" I screamed, the door opened on it's own. It was dark out there. An eerie feeling came over me.

"This can't be happening. This is what I get for watching so many horror movies"

… I heard it again

Knock, knock

"Where the hell is it coming from now" I looked around the room

Knock, knock

"Fuck" I hesitated to move closer to the door.

I moved with a sudden turn almost catching whiplash on my neck. I heard a whisper coming from behind me.

Momma always told me to never respond when my name is being whispered, I'm ignoring that"

I turned back around and came face to face with a dark figure. When if realized I saw it, it darted across the doorway.

"Jesus Christ what the hell was that?"

Snapchat notification

J – "Are you ok?"

Me – "Hell no I'm scared shitless, I don't know what's going on but you need to GET HERE FAST!!!"

J – "I'm a few blocks away"

Close Snapchat

"I need to get out of here" I grabbed my fanny pack, keys and phone and walked out of my room. Bad idea.

Towards my apartment door stood a dark figure. It was tall, had long arms almost touching the floor, razor sharp fingers and it was breathing hard through its teeth.

"Oh shit" I ran back into my room and locked the door. I ran to the fire escape, that was the only exit I had.

I heard it knock again.

Knock, knock

Open Snapchat

Video call Jamil

Me – "Where are you?!"

J – "I'm pulling up to your building right now"

I looked down and saw his gray car double park in front of my apartment building.

"Oh Thank God"

I saw Jamil run up and go inside the building.

Video call

J – "What apartment you live in?"

Me – "53, please be careful, its trying to come into the room"

I was genuinely frightened. I was trembling all over, sitting in a corner out in the fire escape. I just prayed it didn't come out here.

J – "I'm coming"

He stood with me on the phone until he made it up here. He ran up the stairs and stood in front of my apartment door.

J – "I'm here, the door is unlocked" he showed me that it was slightly open.

Me – "I didn't unlock it"

J – "I'm coming in, where are you?"

Me – "On the fire escape"

He walked in, all I saw was pure darkness. He walked slowly, I could hear his footsteps. I saw something in front of him.

Me – "Be careful, I just saw something" I whispered

J – "What did you say?" he whispered back

He heard something shuffling in front of him.

"What the hell?"

I ran in from the fire escape, I opened my room door and dragged him inside and shut the door back up. I hugged him tight, he hugged me back.

Knock, knock

"What the fuck?" he asked

"It's trying to mess with us but I can't tell where the knocking is coming from"

"Wait, do you hear that?' Jamil asked

A low growl came from somewhere in the room. We stood closer together, looked around the room and saw nothing. Another growl, this time I heard it come from the mirror.

Knock, knock

Jamil made the mistake of getting closer to the mirror.

"Nooo, wait.. "

Suddenly the mirror shattered, Jamil fell back, luckily able to cover his face before it completely cut him.

"Shit!" he yelled

A dark shadow crept out of the hole that was once a mirror.

"Come on let's go" I grabbed him, we ran out of my room, the door slammed and then a loud booming voice came from all over the apartment.

"GET OUT"

It was so loud the we ducked and covered our ears. We heard a loud rolling thunder come from above us and then it stopped.

A whisper came from the left side of my ear... "Run"

I grabbed Jamil's arm and hauled ass. Heard the door slam and lock. We ran down the stairs, saw one of my neighbors and quickly said, "Tell the landlord I left and my roommates and I aren't coming back, my apartment is haunted, don't go up there."

Got into Jamil's car and drove off.

(Neighbor)

"Haunted? Seriously?" shaking his head he curiously took the elevator to the 5th floor. "There's no such thing as a haunted apartment in this building" he continued to speak to himself as he walked towards the apartment.

"She left the door open" he sighed

"Stupid girl probably couldn't afford her rent"

He slowly walks in, nothing but darkness and a eerie feeling. He continued walking in deeper into the apartment.

"Let me snap this, might get some views since is looks so creepy" he admitted sarcastically.

Open Snapchat

"What's up snap, I'm in my neighbors crib right now. She just ran out of here claiming that this place is haunted... oooocuuuuu. She probably left cause she cant pay the rent and used this as an excuse" he continued as he walked.

"Damn, the lights don't work" he said as he tried the light switch. "She ain't pay her Con Ed bill, her broke ass"

Knock, knock

"You came back!" he said as he spun around and saw .. no one.

"Who's there?"

Knock, knock

"I know ya'll heard that, seems like it's coming from this room. Is anyone in here?" he asked again.

Nothing!

He opened the door and saw the shattered mirror and the open window. "what the hell?" he walked over the glass and towards the window.

"Ya'll see this mess? He continued to record on Snapchat.

As he walked towards the window, the bedroom door slowly closed behind him. He closed the window but then felt someone grab him by the back of his neck, pick him up and throw him through the window. His screams were heard and so the loud cracking "thud" on the concrete. Everyone on snap saw it.

The police were called.

All they found was an empty apartment, a shattered mirror, a broken window and the guy's phone by the window sill.

Close Snapchat

The Sanatorium Trip

"I'm so bored!" my son Jeremy expressed to me.

"Can we do something? Go to the pool? The mall? I don't even care where we go, I'm tired of playing Fortnite"

We were forth bored. His dad wasn't around, he was on a baseball trip for a couple of days and Emma was with my mother. I was scrolling through google looking for an idea for my next story when I bumped into this sanatorium I've always wanted to visit. It's out in Louisville, Kentucky and we are allowed to visit and take a tour and explore.

"You feel like taking a trip?" I asked Jeremy

"Hell yea, where we going?" he was ecstatic.

"Weeeeellllllll, there's this haunted sanatorium, like an asylum I've always wanted to go visit and..."

"Wait! Haunted? Seriously? What the heck is wrong with you? Always wanna do scary stuff" he was looking at me all weird.

"And every time we do something scary, don't we always have fun? Stop fronting like if you don't enjoy it" I widely smile.

His face was expressionless, he just stared at me.

"Ok!" he smiled. "Where's this place at and what happened there?"

"I'm glad you asked. We're going to Louisville, Kentucky to the famous Waverly Hill Sanatorium. It used to be a tuberculosis hospital that opened up in 1910".

"A lot of strange things happened there" I began to explain

"Like what?!"

"Well the "Doctor's" that worked there began doing human experiments like putting balloons inside their bodies to expand their lungs and putting the patients in a radiation room because radiation supposedly cleared the tuberculosis going around. It was called the "White Plague".

"Whoever didn't survive these experiments would end up thrown down the "Death Tunnel"

"What the hell?!" his face was priceless

"Right! Apparently there was a faked suicide of a pregnant nurse"

"A faked suicide? How is that possible?"

"Well the nurse got pregnant by one of the doctors, which was frowned upon. The doctor didn't want to be with her after he found out she was with child, tricked her and forced an abortion. The abortion went wrong, she was bleeding to much so he made it seem like she hung herself in room 502 and she bled out"

"Damn, that's cruel, so evil" Jeremy had a look of disgust

"Oh yea, and it's being haunted till this day by a ghost of a young boy named Timmy".

"What the hell? And it's really haunted? Like with real ghost and shit? Like really really??!! Not like the ones we go to for Halloween right?" he rushed his questions excitedly.

"Yea Jay it's real a real haunted hospital, not with actors but with real ghost"

He was thinking.

"Ummmm, I'm not to sure about this now" he shook his head.

"Oh come on , are you serious? You're such a wuss. Now you don't want to go?" I asked him.

He paused for a moment. He sighed.

"Fine, let's go"

"Atta boy!!!" I jumped with joy.

I called my husband and told him that Jeremy and I will be taking a little adventure then we packed our bags and off to Louisville, Kentucky we went.

2 hours and 35 minutes later we landed in Kentucky.

"Jeremy wake up, we're here" I shook him out his sleep, nearly fell off his chair.

"Huh?! What?! Where are we???" he was startled

"We're in Kentucky bozo" I giggled

"Oh.. yea, I forgot"

We boarded off the plane and immediately spotted a black limo and the driver holding sign with our names on it.

"Ooohh snap we boujee now" Jeremy said while snapping his fingers in a Z formation.

I just stared at him. "Don't do that again"

We got into the limo. It was a super comfortable ride. Jeremy had no idea what was coming, this trip was going to be epic. He's going to love it.

We arrived at our destination, at The Waverly Hills Sanatorium.

"This place is huge Jen" he said looking up at the place.

"Hey Jennifer?!" a man dressed very nicely asked.

"Yes?"

"Hi, I'm Mr. Brache, your tour guide for the duration of your stay" he said while looking extravagant.

"Heeeyyy Mr. Brache, my name is Jeremy and this is my mom dukes Jennifer" Jeremy joked.

"Yes, im aware of who you are" Mr. Brache smiled.

"It's Jen.. call me Jen, Mr. Brache"

"Ok, will do. Come join me, I'll introduce you to the rest of the tour and then you guys can go ahead and get settled in".

We walked into Waverly hills and I instantly felt a vibe and it definitely wasn't a good one. I looked around, this place as enormous. It had so may doors and windows, graffiti everywhere, the walls were rusted and the ceilings were stained, it looked like blood. The smell, let's not even talk about the lingering smell of decay, the smell of death.

This place is said to be the most haunted place in America.

"Here, take these" Mr. Brache handed us medical face masks, it's like he knew what I was thinking.

"Oh thank God" Jeremy grabbed the mask and quickly put it over his nose and mouth.

"It smells like death in here" those were my thoughts exactly and that's not a good thing.

Part 2

The tour started at 12:00 am precisely, it was now 11:45pm.

"Come on Jay, hurry the hell up kid"

"Alright, alright I'm coming" he responded. I swear I don't know what to do with this kid, he popped out with a matching Nike outfit.

"Seriously Jay?! We're going on a tour and a possible ghost hunt and this is how you dress?"

"Yea I gotta look fly all time and I might find me a ghost boo! Haha get it? Ghost boo?!" he was smiling a little to hard. "And what do you mean a possible ghost hunt? I thought it was just a tour"

"Yea it is and then while the tour is distracted we're going to go elsewhere and do our own thing. I'm thinking of going to room 502 and doing an investigation in there." I told Jeremy while I finished packing my bookbag with snacks and water.

"Oh I almost forgot this" I picked up my tape recorder. "We're having an EVP session also"

"Jen, what the hell is wrong with you?, what goes through your head?" he asked me while fixing his sneakers.

" I like adventure and I've always wanted to ghost hunt in this place so shut up and lets go"

We made our way to where the other tourist were and waited for Mr. Brache to begin.

It was dim. Sheets on the furniture, broken tables and chairs. The windows well tall, some were cracked from top to bottom. The lights were flickering, making the ambience much more creepy. The staircases were filled with spiderwebs and were gloomy and damp.

That smell was still lingering, the smell of rotten meat, the smell of death. It made my stomach turn all sorts of ways. I also felt a vibe, something was definitely here with us... and it wasn't good.

"Jen!" Jeremy startled me. "The tour is moving, let's go!"

We followed the group. I had to cover my nose with the face mask again because the smell was still terrible. We began touring on the first floor. Mr. Brache showed us one of the many tuberculosis rooms. Mr. Brache explained to us how the patients were tortured by the doctors. The doctors would sometimes insert balloons into the patients bodies to help them breathe. Their ribs and muscle tissues were removed to fit the balloons, this caused many deaths in this place because if the painful and ineffective treatment.

"Something also happened in room 502!" Mr. Brache exclaimed. "That room is said to be haunted by the torn spirit of a nurse. It is said that a nurse had committed suicide here, hung herself with a noose but others say she was murdered by one of the doctor who got her pregnant, conducting an obligated abortion that went extremely wrong. When the nurse was found she had blood dripping from under her gown. So the story of her committing suicide may be false, a cover up to the murder that was committed and now she haunts this room and these hallways. Many people who enter the room feel strange being in it. Be careful.. you may see her tonight."

Mr. Brache continued.

"I'm so excited" Jeremy said. "Really?, I thought you were scared" I asked him.

He sucked his teeth. "I'm a God at ghost hunting"

"Jeremy you're not even a God at Fortnite so stop it" I laughed at the look on his face.

"Oh My God, why are your lying Jen?" his pitch was high, a little to high for my liking.

"First off, you have never been on a ghost hunt so cut it out son and you were scared as hell not so long ago so hush it" I laughed.

"Whatever"

"Good evening everyone" Mr. Brache came up to the tour group. "We're about to begin our tour but before that I have a few rules" Mr. Brache expressed.

"Here we go" I smiled.

"Number one, no flash photography. Yes pictures are allowed, you do what to remember this experience but no flash, you don't want to scare any ghost now do you?" Mr. Brache said with a smirk.

"Number two, no pushing or shoving, you will all get to see the different areas. Last but not least number three, please and I urge you to not abandon the group. This place is pretty dangerous if you travel alone". Mr. Brache had a concerned look on his face, he was serious.

"Well, there goes your adventure!" Jeremy said as he started walking together with the group.

"Let's begin" Mr. Brache started to walk into the sanitorium and so did we. It still had that terrible smell of death. I gagged.e Death Tunnel" everyone looked towards the far end of the hall, it was pitch black on that side. "I don't think we'll hit that place up tonight, to many things happened down there and im not willing to risk my job or your lives just for a little fright"

"BINGO!" I excitedly whispered.

Part 3

"Jen, my stomach is killing me right now, I feel so nauseous" Jeremy was holding his stomach. "Here, drink some water" I handed a bottle of water over to him.

"Aaaaaahhhhh!!!, what the hell?!" I yelled.

"Whaattt??!!! Are you ok?! One of the tourist asked me and he ran towards me.

"I felt something touch my arm but its was really hot, felt like my arm was burning for a moment"

The man lifted my arm and looked at it with disbelief. "Jesus Christ" he whispered.

I had a blistering hand print on my right arm. Looked like it was branded into me. The man took Jeremy's water bottle and pour some water on the print, it sizzled.

"OH MY GOD!!!!" it was so painful. While the man was helping me, behind him I caught a glimpse of something, looked like a shadow dash across the doorway.

"Did you see that?" a woman from the tour asked.

"Yes I did. What the hell was that?!" I asked nervously.

"You're probably seeing things because of the pain". Mr. Brache said.

"How? If we both saw the same shit?" the lady looked at him like if he was dumb or something. "Yea that's true. Jeremy are you ok? You look pretty pale in the face there man" Mr. Brache asked with some concern.

"I feel sick"

I gave Jeremy the water bottle back, he poured some on his face. "I need to throw up" he ran off into a corner and barfed all over the wall.

(Blaaargh, Blaaaargh)

He wiped his mouth and took a swig of water.

"Whew, I feel much better now" he smiled.

"Let's continue with the tour" I suggested while holding my arm

"Are you?, how's your arm?" Mr. Brache asked me.

"Yea, I'm sure, it's just a little sting, I'm fine. Let's go"

We continued with the tour. The more we kept walking the creepier it felt. We then stopped walking and was standing in front of a big door. The smell coming from inside it was putrid. I tried reading the sign above the door, it was the morgue.

"I didn't know this place had a morgue" I whispered to Jeremy.

"Look at what's right next to it though" he pointed at something across from the morgue. It was the Death Tunnel". That was the tunnel where the doctors would throw the failed experiments.

Jeremy walked over to the door of the tunnel and decided to be a smart ass and opened the door. The worst mistake he could of made. We tried to immediately shut the door back up, what we heard was the scariest sounds I have ever heard in my life. It was the voices, whispers and cries of the dead. It was so disturbing. Goosebumps were all over my body. I had to cover my ears because it was so loud.

Jeremy hid behind me while the other men tried to close the door. The screams wouldn't allow to them to shut the door up.

"What's going on Jen?!" Jeremy shouted.

"I think you just released some shit Jay, those are the screams of the dead"

"

We've never experienced this before" Mr. Brache yelled my way.

"ALRIGHT THAT'S GREAT, NOW CLOSE THE DOOR!!!" Jeremy shouted over the screams.

The men managed to all work together and shut the tunnel door shut. The screams stopped.

"Oh thank God" I breathe out.

"I think we should call it a night and end the tour early, to many strange things happening and we're not even half way done" Mr. Brache suggested to the tour group.

"WHAT?! NO WAY! Let's keep going, we got this" Jeremy stomped his foot.

"No kid, I think we're done for tonight, plus your mom's arm doesn't look so good, she's got to take care of that as soon as possible"

I looked at my arm and it was indeed getting worst. We began to walk down the hallway towards the exit of the sanatorium. I hadn't realize how far we actually walked into this place.

"What the?" I whispered to myself, startled.

"What happened?" Jeremy looked at me and asked.

"Nothing, I thought I saw something move down there".

Mr. Brache walked upfront and stopped dead on his tracks. He was staring up ahead slowly moving his head from in front of him to above him. We all followed his gaze.

"I don't see anything but ugh there goes that smell again" a lady from the tour group expressed. It suddenly got really cold, so cold that we were able to see our breaths in front of us.

"Jesus! What the hell?!" I said covering my nose and mouth.

A dark shadow, looked more like smoke was traveling above us. We all duct down. Suddenly we heard chocking. One of the men in the tour group was chocking. His hands were clutching his throat but something else was choking him. He was actually chocking on the smoke, it was going into his mouth and his nose. He couldn't even scream.

"Oh my God somebody help him"

The man suddenly dropped on the floor like a sack of potatoes. He wasn't moving, he wasn't breathing. The smoke vanished into thin air.

"WHAT WAS THAT?" Mr. Brache yelled after the watching that thing disappear.

"I believe that that was the spirit or something far more worst" I responded.

"Let's get out of here, fast!" Jeremy said walking away from us.

Suddenly we all covered our ears and yelled. All the doors sudden slammed shut at the same time. "You've got to be kidding me" I sighed, put my bookbag on the floor and opened it.

"Jeremy here, take this and turn it on."

"What is this?" he questioned me on the object in his hand, looking at it strangely.

"It's an EVP reader" I responded back and snatched it from him, turned it on and placed it on the floor.

"What the hell is an EVP?"

"Bro, really? It's an Electronic Voice Phenomenon. It records the dead talking."

"Oh shit" he exclaimed.

"What do you intend on doing with that thing?" Mr. Brache asked.

"This isn't the time for games lady" a man from the group sneered.

"Watch how you talk to my mother aight?" Jeremy sounded threatening.

"It's ok Jay, he wouldn't understand"

I sat in front of the EVP recorder, pressed record and began talking. "Is anyone here with us? If there is please turn on the flashlight" I had also set a small flashlight next to the recorder. We waited a moment for a response. NOTHING!

I asked again. "Is anyone here with us? If so please turn on the flashlight."

Suddenly, I caught a chill. "Do you feel that?" Jeremy asked. He fet the cold creeping up his arm. "Yeah I felt it too" Mr. Brache chimed in. We all patiently waited but I don't know what we were waiting for.

"You gotta be kidding me" another person from the tour group stated. "I know you're not waiting for the light to ... OUCH! What the fuck?!" the man yelled in pain. The flashlight turned on. It was shinning against the wall, there was a shadow forming against it.

"What the hell?" Mr. Brache whispered. The flashlight then shut off.

"We gotta go, whatever is here isn't good" I packed up my belongings and headed towards the exit.

A loud **BOOM** came from all around us, it sounded like all of the doors in the sanitorium slammed shut. We all screamed and covered

our ears and heads, we were scared out of our minds. "What is happening here?" someone asked.

We looked around us, everyone was safe but the atmosphere felt different. It felt dark.. Evil!

"Guy's. we have to go **NOW"**

"Jen, what's happening?" Jeremy asked me as we tried walking away. I looked at him and lowered my head. "I did something stupid before we came here, you were in the shower" I admitted.

"Oh God , what did you do?" he asked me

I wasn't ready to tell him but I had to, I had no choice.

"i came here earlier, alone and played with a Ouija Board. I tried to communicate with someone and I think I did but whoever it was didn't want to let me say good-bye, some shit was with me in the room. I was in room 502"

"You are not normal" the look on Jeremy's face was priceless.

"I wanted to see if It was really haunted. Remember that's what we actually came for and prove that it really is"

I smiled but that soon faded away. I quickly turned around because I heard footsteps running but saw no one.

"Come on, we have to leave this place"

Jeremy stopped walking. "Did you hear that?

"Hear what?"

"Shhh, listen" he said.

"I didn't hear anything" I whispered.

"I heard someone calling me" he was looking at the long, dark corridor behind us.

"It came from there" he pointed in the direction.

"Do you see that? Who is that?" he was backing away from me, he was scared of whatever was coming towards us.

I saw what he was looking at. It was a girl with a long white, dirty dress, long black hair that covered most of her face. Whatever lights were still on around us flickered with every step she took.

"RUN!" I yelled.

We ran the opposite direction towards the group and ran past them.

"She's comiiinnggg" we ran past the group.

"Who's coming?" Mr. Brache asked. He turned the direction we came from and was violently grabbed from his neck, picked up into midair and was dropped abruptly like a sack of potatoes.

"Oh my God Mr. Brache" a lady yelled. Jeremy and I stopped running. We didn't see that thing, that girl anymore. We were breathing hard. My head was beginning to hurt. "Come on jay, let's go help"

I began to do chest compressions on Mr. Brache for a few minutes until he began breathing and coughing.

"What the hell happened?" he was coughing and massaging his neck. "Who's coming?"

I gave him a concerned look. I was panicking on the inside.

"Zozo"

Part 4

"A while back my friends and I decided to be idiots and play around with a Ouija board" I began to explain to the tour group while trying to figure out how to get out of this place.

"We opened up a portal, a gate to something and the Ouija board demon responded to us. He showed up in human form and killed a few of my friends but now its after me again."

Everyone just stared at me confused and angry. A lady ran up on me and tried hitting me. "Bitch try that shit again and watch you not get back up" I yelled at her.

"I already contacted my best friend, she's on her way as we speak as of a few hours ago. She'll get us out."

A gust of cold, chilled air came over us. "It's here! Let's go".

We quickly started walking towards the exit again and suddenly stopped. The girl that Jeremy and have had seen before was standing by what it looked like our only way out.

"is that it?" Jeremy asked, his voice trembling.

"That's a huge possibility my son."
It just stared at us, the girl or whatever it was. I started to feel strange, my chest was tight, I couldn't breathe. Everyone else was frozen in place. She's controlling us.

The look in her eyes was so .. Sinister.

I started to panic making it harder for me to concentrate.

"oh my God Rebz, where are you?" I screamed in my head. Tears were rolling down my face.

The girl just vanished into this air. Just vanished, turned into dust. We all were released from the girl's grasp and fell to the floor panting hard.

"She's here!" I ran to the exit.

"Who's here now?!" Jeremy ran after me trying to catch his breath.

"My best friend!"

Outside of Waverly Hills sat my best friend Rebeca. She was kneeling down a few feet away from the building with an open book. Her hands in prayer form, her hair was flowing wild. She began to rock back and forth. Blood began to trickle down her nose.

Inside Waverly Hills the floor began to tremble.

"What hell is going on?" Jeremy shouted over the noise.

"I think it's Rebeca, whatever she's doing is making this happen." The trembling finally stopped. We looked around, the air felt different. We heard a door open up and some light shone in.

"Jen?!" Rebeca's voice was heard.

"Jen, where are you?"

"I'm right here" I ran to her and hugged her so tight, she felt cold.

"Thank you so much for saving us Rebz"

"It was my pleasure" I looked at her, she smiled. I backed away from her.

"Run"

"What?!, Why?!" Jeremy and everyone else backed away with me.

"That's not Rebeca"

"How can you tell?" Mr. Brache asked.

"Her eyes, they were bright yellow, they were demon eyes"

Rebeca or who I thought was Rebeca disappeared from behind us and appeared in front of us making us all slam against some sort of invisible wall. Rebeca randomly pushed the tour group against the sanatorium wall. Feet off the floor, not able to move a muscle. I stood alone facing her. Her yellow eyes dug into my soul.

"I came here for you, you called me and I'm back" she said.

"Zozo?!"

"In the flesh" she grinned an evil grin.

Jeremy was trying his hardest to move. He was forcing his hand to move into his pocket.

"We have some unfinished business to take care of" Rebeca or should I say Zozo grimaced.

"We have no business, so go back to the hell hole you came from"

"Sweety, you opened up that portal, you're the only one that can close it but I won't allow you to" Zozo said.

She began walking closer to me, her hair was slowly floating like static. She brushed it down with her hands. The lights above us flickered a little. We looked up and then at each other. She gave me a strange look.

"What's going on?" she looked perplexed.

"Huh?"

She walked towards me and then just stopped. Black smoke started to rise from her feet. She was trying to brush the smoke off with her hand but it wasn't working.

She looked up at me, I smiled.

Jeremy suddenly released himself off the wall, he was panting for air. While he was on his knees he looked up at the human form of Zozo and charged at her, knocking her down and letting out a scream.

"Aaaaahhhh, you BITCH" he punches her on the face and her face sizzles. Jeremy was holding the crucifix I had given him before we came on this trip. It was blessed with holy water. She screams a horrific, painful scream. While she screamed, Jeremy poured holy water down her throat. She burned.

Her insides were smoking, her eyes were a mix of yellow and red. Her screams were ear piercing.

"I'LL BE BACK" Zozo screamed before she disintegrated into the air.

"Holy shit" Jeremy yelled. "I did it! I got rid of her" he got up from where she was laying and kicked the leftover ashes. "Bitch"

Part 4

Static on the television screen

News Announcer - "In today's paranormal news, a tour guide and a group went to the famous

Waverly Hills Sanatorium, where no one came out alive except for one lady and her son who remained the only survivors in this tragic accident. Apparently the Ouija board demon Zozo appeared at Waverly Hills and dismembered the entire tour group. The mother and son got away.

"Look Jeremy, we made the newspaper headlines too" I was all excited. Jeremy didn't look at me though, he kept starring at the television.

"Jeremy! I'm talking to you"

He slowly got up from his seat and turned around to look at me, his eyes were glowing yellow.

"I'm not Jeremy"

Personal Experience #3

During this school year (2019) a student, his paraprofessional and myself were standing in the hallway of the school having a conversation about random things when we suddenly stopped talking. I froze place. I asked my co-worker if he heard the same thing I heard and he said yes. The student was shocked as well. What we heard was impossible to hear due to how thick the ceiling of the school and by how many layers it has. We heard what sounded like someone running from one side of the hall to right above room 216, which is my boss office. The running was really fast and hard, like if someone was stomping. Gave me goosebumps. A few seconds after we heard the running, one of the teachers that was meeting with my boss came out the office and asks me, "Jen, who's playing with the door? I said "No one, why?" she replied back saying that someone opened up the door twice while they were meeting. We all looked at each other, baffled.

Two Lines Of Horror

Scared

She ran through the forest. She ran scared away from it.

She saw shadows and heard whispers.

She stopped running, it was right behind her..

It

It watches me through the crack of my closet door. It watches me through the cracks on the floor. It watches me through my window at night. I watch it with such fright.

Me

I looked at myself in the bathroom mirror. Washed my face, fixed my hair but my reflection's face wasn't wet. It stared back at me then blinked.

End.

Made in the USA
Middletown, DE
09 November 2022